Illustrations copyright © 1986 by Daniel San Souci
All rights reserved including the right of reproduction in whole or in part in any form.
Published by LITTLE SIMON/JULIAN MESSNER Divisions of Simon & Schuster, Inc.
Simon & Schuster Building, Rockefeller Center, 1230 Avenue of the Americas, New York, New York 10020.
LITTLE SIMON, JULIAN MESSNER and colophons are trademarks of Simon & Schuster, Inc.
Designed by Sylvia Frezzolini.
Manufactured in Spain.
1   2   3   4   5   6   7   8   9   10 (tr.)

1   2   3   4   5   6   7   8   9   10 (lib.)

Library of Congress Cataloging in Publication Data
Mother Goose.
The Mother Goose book.

Includes index.
Summary: An illustrated collection of well-known nursery rhymes.
1. Nursery rhymes.   2. Children's poetry.
[1. Nursery rhymes]   I. San Souci, Daniel, ill.
II. Title.
PZ8.3.M85 1986d   398'.8   86-18548
ISBN 0-671-62913-1
0-671-63659-6 (lib. ed.)

The Mother Goose Book

A Collection of Nursery Rhymes

Illustrated by Daniel San Souci

Little Simon
Published by Simon & Schuster, Inc.

Jack be nimble,
Jack be quick,
Jack jump over
The candlestick.

Hector Protector was dressed all in green;
Hector Protector was sent to the Queen.
The Queen did not like him,
No more did the King;
So Hector Protector was sent back again.

The Queen of Hearts
She made some tarts,
All on a summer's day;
The Knave of Hearts
He stole the tarts,
And took them clean away.

The King of Hearts
Called for the tarts,
And beat the knave full sore;
The Knave of Hearts
Brought back the tarts,
And vowed he'd steal no more.

Dickery, dickery dare,
The pig flew up in the air;
A man in brown
Soon brought him down,
Dickery, dickery dare.

Rub-a-dub-dub,
Three men in a tub,
And who do you think they be?
The butcher, the baker,
The candlestick-maker,
Turn 'em out, knaves all three!

Old Mother Goose
When she wanted to wander,
Would ride through the air
On a very fine gander.

Mother Goose had a house,
'Twas built in a wood,
Where an owl at the door
For sentinel stood.

Hickety, pickety, my black hen,
She lays eggs for gentlemen;
Gentlemen come every day
To see what my black hen doth lay.
Sometimes nine and sometimes ten,
Hickety, pickety, my black hen.

High diddle, diddle,
The cat and the fiddle,
The cow jumped over the moon;

The little dog laughed
To see such craft,
And the dish ran away with the spoon.

Oh dear, what can the matter be?
Dear, dear, what can the matter be?
Oh dear, what can the matter be?
Johnny's so long at the fair.

He promised to buy me a fairing to please me,
And then for a kiss, oh, he vowed he would tease me,
He promised to bring me a bunch of blue ribbons
To tie up my bonny brown hair.

And it's oh dear, what can the matter be?
Dear, dear, what can the matter be?
Oh dear, what can the matter be?
Johnny's so long at the fair.

He promised to bring me a packet of posies,
A garland of lilies, a garland of roses,
A little straw hat, to set off the blue ribbons
That tie up my bonny brown hair.

Humpty Dumpty sat on a wall,
Humpty Dumpty had a great fall.
All the king's horses
And all the king's men
Couldn't put Humpty together again.

Little Tommy Tittlemouse
Lived in a little house;
He caught fishes
In other men's ditches.

There was an old woman who lived in a shoe,
She had so many children she didn't know what to do.

She gave them some broth without any bread;
She whipped them all soundly and put them to bed.

Christmas is coming,
The geese are getting fat,
Please put a penny
In an old man's hat.

If you haven't a penny,
A ha'penny will do,
If you haven't a ha'penny,
Then God bless you.

Cold and raw the north wind doth blow
Bleak in the morning early,
All the hills are covered with snow,
And winter's now come fairly.

Old King Cole
Was a merry old soul,
And a merry old soul was he;
He called for his pipe,
And he called for his bowl,
And he called for his fiddlers three.

As I was going to St. Ives,
I met a man with seven wives;
Each wife had seven sacks,
Each sack had seven cats,
Each cat had seven kits;
Kits, cats, sacks, and wives,
How many were going to St. Ives?

Sing a song of sixpence,
A pocket full of rye;
Four-and-twenty blackbirds
Baked in a pie.

When the pie was opened,
The birds began to sing;
Wasn't that a dainty dish
To set before the king?

The king was in his counting-house,
Counting out his money;
The queen was in the parlor
Eating bread and honey.

The maid was in the garden,
Hanging out the clothes,
When down came a blackbird
And pecked off her nose.

I saw a ship a-sailing,
A-sailing on the sea,
And oh but it was laden
With pretty things for thee.

There were comfits in the cabin,
And apples in the hold;
The sails were made of silk,
And the masts were all of gold.

The four-and-twenty sailors,
That stood between the decks,
Were four-and-twenty white mice
With chains about their necks.

The captain was a duck
With a packet on his back,
And when the ship began to move
The captain said Quack! Quack!

Jerry Hall,
He is so small,
A rat could eat him
Hat and all.

Needles and pins,
Needles and pins,
When a man marries,
His trouble begins.

Jack and Jill
Went up the hill,
To fetch a pail of water;

Jack fell down,
And broke his crown,
And Jill came tumbling after.

Peter, Peter, pumkin eater,
Had a wife and couldn't keep her;
He put her in a pumpkin shell,
And there he kept her very well.

Polly put the kettle on,
Polly put the kettle on,
Polly put the kettle on,
We'll all have tea.

Sukey take it off again,
Sukey take it off again,
Sukey take it off again,
They've all gone away.

Little Miss Muffet
Sat on her tuffet,
Eating her curds and whey;
Along came a spider,
Who sat down beside her
And frightened Miss Muffet away.

There was an old woman
Lived under a hill,
And if she's not gone
She lives there still.

Baked apples she sold,
And cranberry pies,
And she's the old woman
That never told lies.

Mary, Mary quite contrary,
How does your garden grow?

With silver bells and cockle shells,
And pretty maids all in a row.

Jack Sprat could eat no fat,
His wife could eat no lean.
And so, between them both, you see,
They licked the platter clean.

Barber, barber, shave a pig,
How many hairs to make a wig?
Four-and-twenty, that's enough,
Give the barber a pinch of snuff.

Rain, rain, go away,
Come again another day.

Twinkle, twinkle, little star,
How I wonder what you are!
Up above the world so high,
Like a diamond in the sky.

Index of First Lines